The Adventures of
ABBY and the SEAHORSE
swim the English Channel

BETH PHILLIPS

To order additional copies of this book, contact:
Xlibris
844-714-8691
www.Xlibris.com
Orders@Xlibris.com

ISBN: Softcover   978-1-6698-0877-0
       EBook   978-1-6698-0876-3

Print information available on the last page

Rev. date: 01/25/2022

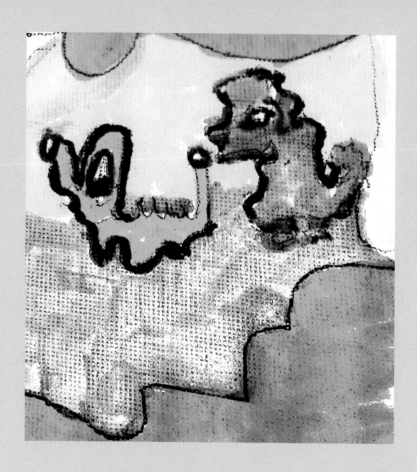

This book belongs to

_____

Grateful acknowledgements to the Conqueror Challenge app and Star Island Resort.

Day one: Abby and the seahorse swim all day from sunrise to sunset and get some help from the love birds Star and Island in terms of a battery operated flashlight that provides light when it gets dark.

Day two: The next day Abby and the Seahorse encounter rain. Nothing will stop them from finishing their goal. That night they stop for healthy food. Healthy food of green apples, bananas and broccoli.

Day three: The Love birds provide music for energy for Abby and the Seahorse. Later that morning the Love Birds pray for Abby and the Seahorse to finish their goal of swimming the English Channel. And sure enough later that day they do.

Day four: Sunrise and later that morning the Love Birds pray for Abby and the Seahorse to finish their goal of swimming the English Channel. And sure enough later that day they do.

Printed in the United States
by Baker & Taylor Publisher Services